THE
CHALICE
OF
LIMERICK

MICHAEL FLANNERY

ISBN 978-1-63630-706-0 (Paperback)
ISBN 978-1-63630-707-7 (Digital)

The sketches in this book were created by Harold Adcock from Madison, Mississippi. The pictures were taken by the author.

Covenant Books, Inc.
11661 Hwy 707
Murrells Inlet, SC 29576
www.covenantbooks.com

To the memory of the Irish priests who have served so faithfully in the original Diocese of Natchez, Mississippi, later known as the Diocese of Natchez-Jackson

It covered the whole state of Mississippi. In 1977, the Diocese of Biloxi was created from the seventeen counties in the south of Mississippi, leaving the Diocese of Jackson to cover the rest of the state.

INTRODUCTION

The Chalice of Limerick is a historical novel. The novel gives an overview of a very difficult time in the history of the Irish nation. Being an overview, it is not intended to be a documentary history of the time. The author will be the first to admit there are gaps in the historical account presented. While it is based on historical facts, the author has chosen to weave into the history other stories which indicate the tenacity of a people who were determined to survive mainly because of a deep-rooted faith in a God who would see them through it. Therefore, I took the liberty to exaggerate the importance of the Chalice of Limerick which was symbolic to a suffering people who were willing to grasp at anything that would offer them a sense of hope in desperate times. Thus, the story of the Chalice of Limerick came into being.

It is my hope that you will enjoy paging through this book. Hopefully, it will inspire you to live your own faith with a little more determination, knowing that others who have preceded you were willing to do the same. The people who have gone before us have been an inspiration and made us who we are today. We owe them a debt of gratitude.

Be who God meant you to be and you will
set the world on fire. (Catherine of Siena)

Bishop O'Brien's Chalice

St. Munchin's Catholic Church, built 1827

Scattery Island, Shannon Estuary

Probably the darkest days in the history of Ireland began with the rise to power of Oliver Cromwell. Thomas Cromwell had been his great, great granduncle. Thomas had been lord chancellor of England from 1532 to 1540 during the reign of King Henry VIII of England. He was one of Henry VIII's chief advisor. Nevertheless, he ended up in the Tower of London and was beheaded on a trumped-up charge of treason. Oliver Cromwell, his great, great grandnephew, was born in Huntington, England, on April 25, 1599. He proved himself to be a great military leader and a general in the English army.

After the execution of King Charles, king of England, (January 30, 1649) through an act of British Parliament, Oliver Cromwell was empowered to go to Ireland; and he put the whole country under siege. He arrived in Dublin with 12,000 soldiers on August 15, 1649. His first stop was Drogheda. Drogheda is just south of Dublin. It had a reputation of being heavily fortified. While the siege lasted only eight days, it resulted in the deaths of 2,000 combatants and 500 civilians. These are conservative estimates. The siege began September 2, 1649. At one point in the siege, a few priests and soldiers barricaded themselves in the steeple of St. Peter's Catholic Church and were burned alive by the Parliamentary soldiers. Any other priests found in the town were clubbed to death.

The next siege began in Wexford to the south of Drogheda on October 2, 1649, and lasted nine days. It was being defended by an estimated 4,800 soldiers, and the attack force numbered about 6,000. Two thousand Royalists/Irish Confederates were killed together with 1,500 civilians. Of the attack forces, only twenty were estimated to have been killed. This was followed by the Siege of Waterford. It took place in two parts. The first siege of Waterford was from October 15 to November 5, 1649. Because of bad weather, the siege was eventually abandoned by the Parliamentary forces. The second siege began in July the following year. Because of the bubonic plague which was responsible for the deaths of 400 people a week within the city, the defending force was reduced to a mere 700 soldiers and 500 pounds of gunpowder. Nevertheless, they did put up a gallant fight. In the meantime, Kilkenny had fallen in March of 1650. The Siege of

Clonmel took twenty-one days. Eventually, the city surrendered. All was not going well for Oliver Cromwell, and the British Parliament wanted his return to England to deal with problems at home. He left his son-in-law (Henry Ireton) in charge and returned to England in May 1650.

The Siege of Limerick took place in two parts. The first siege began in October 1650. Because of bad weather, Henry Ireton abandoned the siege and retreated to his fortress in Kilkenny. He returned the following June. From June 3, 1651, to October 27, 1651, the city of Limerick was under siege. Henry Ireton decided to cut off all supplies to the city and starve the people into surrendering. Henry Ireton had 8,000 under his command, and the city was being defended by Hugh O'Neill and what was left of the Royalists and Irish Confederates. The second siege began on June 3, 1651, and went on until the surrender of the city on October 27, 1651. In the meantime, the plague had taken its toll. It is estimated that 2,000 of the Parliamentary forces died, as well as 700 of the Irish Confederates and close to 5,000 civilians. Henry Ireton himself died on November 26, 1651, as the result of the plague. The mayor of Limerick, Dominic Fannon, was drawn, quartered, and decapitated. The bishop of Limerick, Turlough O'Brien, was hanged for his involvement in the defense of his city and his people.

The Act of Settlement took place in 1652. According to this decree, anyone who fought against the Irish Parliament during the civil wars, if they surrendered within a given time frame, would save their lives but would forfeit up to two-thirds of their lands. Especially, Cromwell wanted to punish Irish Catholics for the rebellion in 1641 and for killing of Protestant settlers particularly in Ulster, the northern province of Ireland.

Before he was captured, Bishop O'Brien entrusted his chalice to his secretary, Father James Kelly. Father Kelly was hiding in the attic of the bishop's home when the Parliamentary forces arrived. They arrested the bishop but never thought to search the attic. He stayed there for two days. In the early hours of the morning of November 1, he made his escape. His first thought was the safety of the chalice. He would bring it to his home in Parteen, three miles away. The egress roads from Limerick City were heavily guarded by the Parliamentary forces. There were checkpoints every mile. Father Kelly decided on another route.

His intention was to cross to the Shannon River at the Thomond Bridge. However, it was being guarded by Parliamentary soldiers. He made his way downstream to the Abbey River and swam across the Shannon River. In his favor, the river was at low tide. He was aware that the passage would not be easy. It was November, and the water would be cold. His destination was the Catholic Church of St. Munchin. St. Munchin's Church had a long history. It was originally built in 561. It was later destroyed by the Danes and rebuilt again. Saint Munchin was the first bishop of Limerick, and he is buried in the church's grounds. The present church overlooks the Shannon River and was built in 1827. Incidentally, in front of the church was later constructed the Treaty of Limerick Stone, marking the end of the nine-year Williamite War. It was signed on October 3, 1691. It is alleged that the agreement was signed on top of the stone.

Father Kelly was sure he would get a change of clothes from the pastor there and then make his way to Parteen, where his family resided, and he could keep the chalice safe there at least for the moment.

As it turned out, he just made it out in time. That same day, the Parliamentary forces returned and ransacked the bishop's home in search of the chalice. Father Kelly was afraid that the Parliamentary soldiers would come to his family home in search of the chalice. They would have been aware of the close association between Bishop O'Brien and Father Kelly. He decided it's best to get it out of town.

Peat or turf was the commodity mostly used to keep the home fires burning in Ireland. It was not unusual for the turf boats to make their way from Kilrush to Limerick to sell the turf. Kilrush is forty miles to the west of Limerick and close to the mouth of the Shannon River. These boats were sailboats capable of carrying up to twenty tons of turf or peat. They would dock at Arthur's Quay and sell the turf to the townspeople. Father Kelly approached the owner of one of these boats and asked him if he would transport Bishop O'Brien's chalice to safekeeping on Scattery Island. Scattery Island is located just two miles from Kilrush on the Shannon Estuary. It has a long history. Originally, it was home to Saint Senan who lived on the island. He was named a bishop sometime between the years 535 and 540. At the time, his jurisdiction covered Limerick, all of County Clare, and parts of County Kerry. Scattery Island had the ruins of a monastery, round tower, and five chapels. There were few families living on the island and a perfect place to hide a chalice for safekeeping.

Father Kelly's plan was that the turf boat would bring the chalice to Kilrush. The captain of the boat was to give the chalice to Thomas Brennan who was a resident of Scattery Island, and he was a second cousin of Father Kelly. Thomas Brennan was to bring the chalice to Scattery Island via a curragh. Curragh boats consisted of a light wooden frame over which were stretched animal skins and sewed together. Today canvas is used. Thomas Brennan considered it an honor to house the bishop's chalice and promised that he would guard it with his life.

There was no resident priest on Scattery Island. For the few families that lived on the island, they would cross the River Shannon on Sundays and attend Mass in the town of Kilrush. During the winter months with bad weather, the passage across the river on the curragh was not possible. During those Sundays, the resident families on Scattery Island would gather in the Brennan household and recite the rosary in the presence of the bishop's chalice. The chalice was a reminder to them of the Eucharistic liturgy. Five years was to pass before Father Kelly would come to Scattery Island to retrieve Bishop O'Brien's chalice.

These were hard times for the citizens of Ireland. Between the years of 1641 and 1652, the population of Ireland was reduced by 20 percent. Injuries suffered in the various sieges were the cause of some of the deaths. Some of this was due in part to the bubonic plague. The bubonic plague is caused by infected fleas. The symptoms are chills, fever, headache, and weakness. The bacteria spreads to the lymph nodes which causes them to swell. There were no medications to ward off these infections.

Irish Catholics faced martyrdom for the practice of their faith. Yet they were ready to make all kinds of sacrifices. Artifacts like the

Chalice of Limerick became a sign and symbol of loyalty to their faith. They were aware of the martyrdom of Bishop Turlough O'Brien, and they drew strength from this fact. After Father Kelly had retrieved the chalice from Scattery Island, he had entrusted it to his mother for safekeeping. One day, soldiers raided her home. At the time of the raid, the chalice happened to be stored in the attic of her bungalow home. The attic could be accessed from the front hallway. Father Kelly's mother put a bucket of milk deliberately in the hallway, and as soldiers were passing in and out, she kept shouting, "Mind my bucket of milk!" As a result, the soldiers never noticed the access to the attic. The soldiers kept looking down at the bucket of milk, and the chalice was safe again.

THE CHALICE ON THE MOVE

The Treaty Stone, Limerick, signed October 3, 1691

Curragower Falls and St. Munchin's Catholic Church

Father Kelly went to Scattery Island to fetch Bishop O'Brien's chalice in 1666. He was given a ride on one of the turf boats from Kilrush which came to Limerick. Father Kelly wanted to visit Scattery Island himself since he had never been there but had heard so much about it. It was an opportunity for him to visit his cousins, the Brennen family, who lived on the island. He would return to Limerick via a turf boat. On the passage back to Limerick on the turf boat, they were stopped by a British patrol boat searching for guns or hidden rebels. The quick thinking of the captain saved the day. He had seen the patrol boat approaching, and he hid the chalice in a burlap sack. He tied a rope around it and threw it into the River Shannon. The other end of the rope was tied to the stern of the turf boat. After inspecting the turf boat, the patrol officers never noticed the rope trailing from the stern of the turf boat. The chalice was safe again.

There seemed to be no end to ongoing conflict in Ireland. Four hundred priests had been captured and deported by 1689. There was no Catholic archbishop in the country from 1692–1714. The price on a priest's head was £5. Still, priests and bishops made their way around the country serving the people. Bishop Patrick Donnelly, bishop of Dromore in 1697, went around his diocese disguised as a harpist. Later a ballad was made commemorating his bravery called "The Bard of Armagh." Catholics and Presbyterians were expected to tithe to the Church of Ireland for the support of its clergy, although they were not members of that church.

The Williamite War began on March 12, 1689, and ended on October 3, 1691. The Williamite War was a conflict between the supporters of the deposed Catholic king James II to ensure he would not regain the throne in England, Ireland, and Scotland by military force. The contender was William of Orange, a Protestant. A very decisive battle was fought north of Dublin and called the Battle of the Boyne 1690, when the supporters of King James II were beaten. To this day, July 12 is celebrated yearly as Orange Day, commemorating the victory at the River Boyne. Strangely enough, the pope at the time was a supporter of William of Orange and is said to have celebrated a Mass of Thanksgiving for the victory of William of Orange on hearing the news in Rome of his success.

The Williamite War had its effects on Limerick which brought more unrest to the inhabitants. King William surrounded the city of Limerick in August 1690.

The Chalice of Limerick was hidden in a home in Limerick which was now under siege. There was a grave danger that if the siege was successful, the city would be ransacked and the chalice could be discovered. A decision was made by Father Kelly, present custodian of the chalice, to move it across the Shannon River to Thomondgate. The Thomond Bridge was heavily guarded by British soldiers. The crossing would be made by a curragh just after midnight. The Shannon River drops a thousand feet in a fifteen-mile distance between Killaloe and Limerick. The drop is very noticeable at the Curragower Falls just west of the Thomond Bridge. As they were making the crossing, the curragh capsized, and the chalice fell into the water and sank right in the middle of the falls. The two occupants, Father Ryan and a friend, were swept downstream. Both were good swimmers and made it ashore close to the Wellesley Bridge, also known as Sarsfield Bridge, on the other side of the river. However, they had regrettably lost the Chalice of Limerick in the crossing. The chalice would lay there for eighteen months until after the signing of the Treaty of Limerick on October 3, 1691.

The Williamite War had its effects on Limerick which brought more unrest to the inhabitants. King William surrounded the city of Limerick in August 1690. He had an army of 26,000. There were

25,000 Irish defending the city, but only half of them had arms. King William had ordered an ammunition train to be sent from Dublin complete with cannons and ammunition. In charge of the Irish forces was General Patrick Sarsfield. An informant told him about the train, and he devised a daring plot to intercept it. On August 10, 1690, with 500 horsemen, he stole out of the city at night, going in the opposite direction to the train. He first went northwest for fifteen miles to the town of Killaloe and crossed the River Shannon north of the town. He then made his way southeast to Ballyneety, where the train was stationed the following night. It took him twenty-four hours to make the trip to Ballyneety. In the early hours of the morning of August 11, with little effort, he had overcome the sentries guarding the train; and he blew up the train together with the cannons and ammunition. He returned a hero to Limerick. This caper instilled great hope in the minds of his soldiers and the residents of Limerick. King William was not to be outdone. On August 27, he ordered more supplies and cannons to be shipped from Waterford. With the aid of this new artillery, a breach was made in the defense wall of the city of Limerick. The Williamite soldiers charged in a frontal attack. A bloody battle ensued. It looked like the Williamites would be successful when even the bystanders watching from a safe distance got involved throwing stones and bottles at the Williamite soldiers. It turned the tide of the battle. Two thousand Williamite soldiers were killed with few casualties on the other side.

The siege had lasted three weeks. King William returned to England on August 31, 1690. The Treaty of Limerick was signed on October 3, 1691. In the terms of the signed treaty, the members of the Jacobite army who wished to return to France could do so. Some of these soldiers did return, and that became known as the "Flight of the Wild Geese." Others decided to join the Williamite army. The Jacobite soldiers who wanted to remain in Ireland could stay provided they took an oath of allegiance to King William. The difficulty was the treaty was mostly ignored.

After the signing of the treaty, it was now safe to try to retrieve the chalice from its resting place in the Curragower Falls. It was going to be a daring task. It would be best to do it at high tide. The current would still be strong, and the depth of water would be about nine feet. Nine curraghs took place in the rescue operation. Each curragh had an oarsman and a great swimmer. The oarsman had the responsibility to try to keep the curragh in the same place while the diver searched beneath at the bottom of the falls. After an hour searching, one diver had successfully retrieved the Chalice of Limerick. It was safe again.

Father Kelly was always careful with Bishop O'Brien's chalice. Mostly he kept it hidden away as a precious heirloom. You did not know the day or the hour when the occupying forces could be at your door on some pretext or other. It was not unusual for them to abscond with a precious object such as a chalice. The celebration of Mass in public was tacitly tolerated. However, the safest way for priests was to celebrate Mass in private. Priests were barely tolerated. Since 1607, Catholics were barred from holding public office. In 1652 in the Act of Settlement, Catholics were barred from membership in the Irish Parliament. The majority of Irish landowners had their lands confiscated under the Adventurers Act. In 1666, forty-nine Catholics from County Roscommon signed a letter in support of the pope and protesting their loss of "due liberties" as citizens of Ireland. They were later executed for their treason. Recently, seventeen of these Catholic martyrs were beatified by Pope John Paul II in 1992. Beatification is a step toward eventual canonization, where the person is declared in the state of bliss and worthy of veneration.

With the unrest, the best thing for priests to do was to celebrate Mass in private for the most part. They dressed in civilian clothes so as not to be identified. Most of the sacraments were celebrated in private homes so as not to draw the attention of the occupying forces. They spoke Gaelic, their native language, and were known to the people. They carried with them the essentials for the celebration of the Eucharist. The whole ministry of Father Kelly and for other priests of his day was the same. In 1692, Father Kelly who was now eighty years of age decided that he would have to find a home for Bishop O'Brien's chalice. He had a priest friend in Cappagh, Kilrush, Father Michael Galvin. He entrusted the chalice to him and asked him to take good care of it. Father Galvin was happy to oblige.

Throughout these troubling times, one of the unifying factors favoring the Irish people was the Gaelic language. English was spoken by the occupying forces, and Gaelic was the language of the Irish. All you had to do was to listen with your ear, and you knew whether the person you were speaking with was friend or foe.

There were penal laws in England after the reign of Henry VIII which penalized Catholics for practicing their faith. An example of this was Father Robert Southwall, who was a poet and spiritual writer. He was arrested while celebrating Mass in 1592 and executed for treason in 1595. In Ireland, the Penal Laws became enacted one hundred years later. They began in 1695 and lasted until 1829.

The Code of Penal Laws in Ireland (1695–1829) were aimed at convincing the colonized Irish into becoming converted from the Roman Catholic faith to Anglican. These penal laws, passed by the British Parliament, were not just for Ireland but also included England and Scotland. These laws penalized the practice of the Catholic religion and imposed civil disabilities on Catholics. The Penal Laws included fines and imprisonment for the participation in worship services and severe penalties including death for priests who practiced their faith in England, Ireland, and Scotland. Catholics were denied the right to vote in public elections. They could not hold public office, hold the title of ownership to property, publish Catholic literature, possess religious artifacts, and keep records of baptisms, marriages, and funerals.

With these penal laws, prospective seminarians were smuggled out of Ireland and sent to seminaries in Paris, France, or Rome, Italy. (As an example, Charles Touhy [1754–1828] who later became bishop of Limerick, studied in Bordeaux, Toulouse, and Paris. He was ordained in Paris in 1789). After ordination, these priests were smuggled back into the country again to begin their ministry. This went on the entire period when the Penal Laws were in effect. The safest way for priests to stay alive was to stay on the move constantly. They usually never spent more than one or two days in the same place. It was a hard life to live, yet they were willing to make the sacrifice to keep the Catholic faith alive in Ireland.

Father Michael Galvin who now possessed the chalice of Bishop O'Brien decided to move to Scattery Island on the Shannon Estuary. The reason for this was that he would be able to see the soldiers coming from the mainland in any direction, and he could try to make his escape. Early one morning, he spotted a contingency of British soldiers approaching the island on a curragh. He hid in a vault which was above ground in the cemetery on the island. For two days, the British soldiers searched for him. The island is only 170 acres in size, but they did not find him. After they left, he came out of hiding. When he would minister on the mainland, he usually made his passage across the two miles by curragh at night. He would have someone meet him at a designated time and place. He usually stayed somewhere in the city of Kilrush at someone's home. He was always careful to rotate where he would stay so as not to setup a pattern. During these visits, he would stay two to three days. He would celebrate Mass at a private home which was usually at night. During the day, he would visit the sick. By word of mouth, people always knew where the Mass would be celebrated, and secrecy was of the utmost importance. Priests were held in the highest respect because their lives were constantly on the line. Bishop O'Brien's chalice was getting much use. The Catholics who would gather for Mass were aware that Bishop Turlough O'Brien was martyred for his faith in the aftermath of the Siege of Limerick when he was captured. In a sense, his spirit was still with the people while his chalice was being used for the celebration of the Eucharist.

MASS ROCKS OF IRELAND

For more than a hundred years during the penal times, priests continued to administer the faith to their people. The Penal Laws were an attempt to eliminate the Catholic faith particularly in Ireland. It was the object of the English Parliament to limit the number of bishops ministering in Ireland. If bishops could be removed from their dioceses, it would eventually have the effect of also eliminating priests altogether. Therefore, no new priests would be ordained. Bishops, then, were the primary target of that section of the Penal Laws. The focus then was to cut off the supply of the clergy.

It might take a generation to accomplish what the British Parliament wanted to do, but that was the plan. During this time, several bishops were executed. For example, the archbishop of Cashel and Emily was hanged in 1584. In 1612, the bishop of Down and Connor was executed. The archbishop of Dublin died in prison in 1680. Oliver Plunkett who was archbishop of Armagh and Primate of all Ireland was hanged, drawn, and quartered on July 1, 1681. He was later declared a saint in 1975 by Pope Paul VI. Saint Oliver Plunkett is the patron saint of peace and reconciliation.

The best efforts of the British Parliament were unsuccessful in subduing the Catholic faith in Ireland. From 1650, seminarians were smuggled out of the country. Mostly, they went to Paris, France, or Rome, Italy. After ordination, they returned to the country of their birth and began their priestly ministry. Priests dressed in civilian clothes and mostly that of farmworkers, so they were not noticed. At checkpoints throughout the country, it was not uncommon for constables to check the hands of the people. If someone had soft hands, it would be hard to pass off as a farmworker or tenant farmer. Priests often worked the fields side by side with other workers.

Throughout the whole country of Ireland, you will find Mass rocks. In the Gaelic they were called *Carraig an Aifrinn*. These rocks were in strategic places. There was available a natural shelter, a good view of the surrounding countryside where sentries were posted in the event of a raid by English soldiers. Invariably, the priest wore a veil over his face while celebrating Mass. This was in case some spy might have infiltrated the gathering and could give him away. According to one penal law, the person apprehending a priest upon the conviction of said priest was to be paid a £100. Very seldom did this happen. Most people feared the repercussions imposed by the community on the perpetrator of such a travesty. Mostly, the priest was known to the Catholic congregation and was respected for his sacrifices. Another of the penal laws imposed a fine of £30 for allowing a priest to celebrate Mass in a private home. Yet people would take that risk, hoping not to be caught.

Sometimes these Mass rocks are found in wooded areas. Priority was given to a strategic place where plenty of advance warning could be given in the event of a raid by the constabulary. There was an indomitable defiance on the part of the Irish Catholic majority not to give in to these harsh restrictions being placed on them—no matter what. Effectively, it was illegal for a priest to celebrate Mass, but Masses were celebrated anyway. Another penal law forbade the keeping of records of baptisms, marriages, or any other sacrament performed. Mass rocks are regarded as sacred places by many people. The tradition still goes on today in several parts of the country where people will gather annually at these Mass rock sites to celebrate the profound faith of their forefathers who made so many sacrifices to preserve their Catholic heritage.

In a penal law passed in 1704, priests were required to be registered with the state after June 24, 1704. This requirement included giving the name, date of birth, place of birth, ordination date, present residence, name of parish of assignment, and name of bishop who gave the assignment. It demanded that at the time of registration, the priest would give two securities of £50 to guarantee peaceful behavior and not to embarrass the state in any way. Failure to do so could mean jail or deportation. This law was observed more in the breach than the observance. For the most part, it was ignored.

One story tells about the Mass rock at Rockhill, County Limerick. Father Michael Galvin had transferred the Bishop O'Brien chalice back to Limerick in the early eighteenth century. Father David Saunders was now in possession of the chalice. His family lived in Raheen, a small village close to Limerick City. He was a young priest who was ordained in Rome in 1710. He was scheduled to celebrate Mass at a secret location in Rockhill, some twenty miles away. Usually he celebrated at these rock Masses without vestments. If he had been caught carrying vestments he would have been executed.

He had sent the Bishop O'Brien chalice two days before by a courier who was passing by Raheen. The courier had delivered the chalice to a lady responsible for organizing the Mass and letting the locals know of its time and location. Nobody ever knew the full story, but for some reason, the British soldiers in a fort in nearby Charleville got wind of the Mass taking place at Rockhill. A body of twenty British soldiers was sent to make an intervention. While the British soldiers had the location right, they did not have the right time. They arrived two hours early. As a result, the people coming to the Mass had not congregated. The lady responsible for bringing the Bishop O'Brien chalice saw the British soldiers coming. She dropped the chalice down the water well in the garden at her home in case her home would be raided. The soldiers did raid her home but never found the chalice. Word went through the Rockhill community like wildfire. Nobody turned up for the Mass, and no arrests were made. The Mass was celebrated the following day after the soldiers had left. The lady in question later claimed that the water drawn from the well was always sweeter after the event.

If perchance a chalice had to be transported from one place to another, a common way to do it was via a horse-drawn cart carrying turf. Turf was the most used material for home fires in Ireland at the time, so a horse-drawn cart would not attract too much attention. It would be easy to hide a chalice there or some other artifact that needed transportation.

On another occasion, Father Saunders was to celebrate Mass in Coonagh. This time, he was bringing the chalice with him. He had made prior arrangements for a curragh to meet him where the Abbey River joins the Shannon River. The rendezvous took place as planned. The river was at low tide. When they had begun the crossing, they noticed British soldiers watching them from the riverbank on the Clare side. Instead of going straight across the Shannon as originally planned, they went downstream as far as Coonagh which was three miles away. By the time the soldiers had secured a curragh to give chase, they had made their escape. A curragh is a lightweight boat. When they landed at Coonagh, they carried the curragh to a barn and hid it in the hay. Three days later, they retrieved it when the coast was clear.

They waited on the bank of the River Shannon until a turf boat was passing by; they hitched a ride on the boat. Turf boats were constantly going up and down the Shannon, and no one would take any notice of a turf boat carrying a curragh on deck.

A big factor with the Mass rock celebrations was the weather. These sites were always outdoors. It would be more difficult for people to assemble in inclement weather. Therefore, it was mostly in the summer months that Masses were celebrated at the Mass rocks. During inclement weather, home Masses took place. However, home Masses were always with smaller congregations. It was more dangerous for the host and the celebrant to have home Masses because of the heavy fine of **£30** being imposed on the host if caught. Sometimes the Mass was celebrated in a barn.

After ministering for twenty-five years always on the run, Father Saunders was captured by the British forces. He was en route to celebrate Mass at Birdhill, some fifteen miles from Limerick, when he was caught at a checkpoint set up by the British soldiers. He was making his way there by horseback. He had avoided all the main roads on his journey. It was a back road just two miles from his destination that he was captured. He was brought back to the Limerick garrison in chains. The following day, he was tried for treason. His crime was that he was a priest and, contrary to the Penal Laws, he continued to celebrate Masses. He was found guilty and sentenced to death by hanging. He did not deny that he was a priest. His mother, an old woman, was permitted to visit with him the night before his execution. He secretly told her where he had hidden the Bishop O'Brien chalice, and he instructed her to give it to Father Sean Kennedy, a friend of his. He did tell his mother to be careful in case she was caught with the chalice. He suggested that she would wait two weeks before making her move. He had drawn a rough sketch of its location and told her to consume the piece of paper before she left his cell room, in case she would be searched by the soldiers who were guarding him. Luckily, she had consumed the sketch before the soldiers had searched her. Heartbroken, she was there for his execution, together with his father and his sister. After letting his body hang for a day from the gallows, they allowed the family to bury his remains in the family grave. Father Saunders had died a martyr's death bravely professing his faith in the Lord Jesus.

With the ongoing persecution of the faith of the Catholic people, the custom arose of having family prayer time in households. This would take place usually after the evening meal, and the rosary was a common prayer ritual. People also had the practice of having a sacred space in their home. It may be a picture of the Lord or a statue, but there was one corner which was regarded as sacred in the home. Also, a penal rosary came into common use during the penal times—that is, a rosary with only eleven beads. Ten of those beads represented the prayer Hail Mary and one represents the Our Father. If stopped and searched by a patrol, the lady would invariably reply that the penal rosary was a bracelet. It looked like a bracelet. Sometimes people wore them on their arms.

Another trait of the Irish people is blarney. Blarney is flattery that is applied to a situation so lightly that you love it. If stopped by a British patrol and asked to account for oneself and the respondent had a small bottle of poteen (illegal whiskey made mostly from potatoes), the respondent would reply it is a bottle of "water." The constable, upon tasting the so-called water, would challenge the respondent;

and he would probably respond, "It is a miracle. It is now poteen." Another example of blarney is the story of the widower in his eighties who wanted to marry a widow also in her eighties. When asked for the reason why, he responded that "he needed someone to help him with his night prayers." During the troubled times, an Irishman would never ask a lady directly if she would marry him. His proposal would go like this: "Would you like to be buried with my people?" If she said yes, then they were engaged. If she said no and boasted about how she turned him down, his response would probably be, "I was only offering her a space in the cemetery." In that way, he saved face. If stopped by the constabulary at a checkpoint to know where a man was going at 8:00 a.m., his response might be that he was going to the pub to quench his thirst. If the constable responded saying: "Have you lost your mind? It is only 8:00 a.m." The response would be, "Yes, I have lost my mind and there is a sizeable reward for finding it." Irish people see a difference between blarney and boloney. Blarney is really flattery applied lightly. Boloney is flattery so thick that it is distasteful.

HEDGE SCHOOLS

Christian Brothers Primary School, Limerick, founded 1816

W ith the Penal Laws in force, education of children became increasingly difficult during the penal times. Laws forbidding education really began in 1695. The thrust of the law forbade Catholics and Presbyterians from managing their own schools. There were severe penalties for any parent or guardian who sent any child to the continent to be educated in any school. The law specifically mentioned any abbey, monastery, convent, or seminary. The penalties upon such a conviction were severe such as forfeiture of lands owned by the perpetrators. This restrictive and oppressive law led to the formation of an alternate way of educating children apart from the state-recognized schools which favored the Anglican faith. These schools were called "hedge schools."

The children would meet by hedge groves, thus the name hedge schools. Barns were particularly popular places, as were homes and occasionally the home of the teacher himself. The main thrust of the education was the three Rs: reading, writing, and arithmetic. Some of these schools had remarkable teachers, who went way beyond the normal primary level of education and offered secondary education topics such as history, geography, Latin, and Greek. Depending on availability of students, it was probable to have a wide range of students in one classroom, consisting of two, three, or four grades. There was no real supervision over the instructor teaching the lessons, no inspectors, no timetable, no curricula, or regulations; and these schools were free from government control. The average length of a school year was 132 days. The main reason for this was most students helped their parents harvest the crops at harvest time. These schools continued to be popular all over the country. They offered a viable alternative to the state-run schools which were pro-British and anti-Catholic in their philosophy of education. Some of these teachers had been former seminarians who had not persevered in the pursuit of a priestly vocation. Others were regular trained teachers.

In the mid-1700s, it is estimated that 400,000 children attended these schools. The estimated number of hedge schools was 9,000. Parents paid the teacher what they could in tuition. Some children who worked the land during the day were instructed at nighttime. The law banning hedge schools was eventually removed in 1793, but the hedge schools continued to flourish well into the mid-1800s.

The religious education of children in these schools continued to thrive. The priest was an occasional visitor, but he depended on the teacher and parents for the most part for their religious instruction. Most of these teachers were committed to their faith and considered it an honor to take time to instruct their students in the tenets of the faith.

God moves in mysterious ways. Sometimes He writes straight with crooked lines. Edmund Rice was born in Callen, Kilkenny, on June 1, 1762. He would later have a tremendous effect on the education of the poor. Edmund had been educated by an Augustinian monk in his hometown of Callen. Edmund had an uncle, Michael Rice, in nearby Waterford who invited Edmund to join his expanding business of buying and selling livestock to be shipped from Waterford, a port city, to different British colonies. Edmund became a keen businessman. His uncle died in 1785, and Edmund took over the business. That same year, he got married. After being married for only four years, his pregnant wife, about to give birth, had a serious accident. We can only speculate as to what the accident was. Some claim she fell from a horse. Others say that she was thrown from a carriage after the horses panicked. In any case, following the accident, she gave birth to a daughter who had physical handicaps. Edmund's wife died shortly after the birth of the daughter, probably due to a fever. Edmund was left to raise the handicapped daughter. Later the daughter turned out to have learning disabilities.

Edmund always had a yearning to help the poor and was involved in various outreach programs in Waterford. After the tragic death of his beloved wife, Edmund's first thought was to join a monastery. He was leaning on going to France. One day while discerning what he would do with his life, it was suggested to him by the sister of the bishop of Waterford that he could teach poor children. He was a man of means. He sold his business in 1802 and started a school in a converted stable on New Street, Waterford. It was an instant success. He expanded and started a second school in Stephen Street, Waterford.

Edmund could not do all the teaching himself, so he sought out other young men to join him in his adventure. Meanwhile, two men who were discerning a vocation came to see him. They were in search of a religious order. They were Thomas Grosnenor and Patrick Finn. They decided to stay with Edmund Rice, and they became the first members of his fledging religious order, later to become known as the Congregation of Christian Brothers. They made adaptations to the rule of life lived by the Presentation Sisters of that time. The members of this new religious order would have as a distinctive charism "dedicated to teaching the poor, free of charge." On August 15, 1808, Edmund Rice and six others took their first religious vows before the bishop of Waterford, John Power. They took the normal religious vows common to all: poverty, chastity, and obedience. Their motto would be *Facere et Docere* (To Do and to Teach). It was Edmund's vision for this new religious community to be open to receiving any poor child, irrespective of the religious affiliation of the parents. The Brothers moved into the property owned by Edmund Rice, Mount Sion, Waterford. While taking vows, Edmund took the religious name Ignatius. Saint Ignatius was the founder of another religious order, the Jesuits. These seven religious brothers took their vows before the bishop of Waterford, who gave them official recognition of the Catholic church, and the members were now a diocesan rite religious order under the jurisdiction of the local bishop of Waterford, Ireland. As a religious congregation, the Christian Brothers began to expand rapidly. There was a need to set up schools in other towns such as Kilkenny, Carrick-on-Suir, and Cork. Every time the Congregation of Christian Brothers wanted to set up a new school, it would request the permission of the bishop of Waterford and the bishop of the city within which the new school was to be built. Consequently, in 1820, the Congregation of Christian Brothers sought approval from Pope Pius VII to be recognized as a pontifical rite institute. This would free the Congregation of Christian Brothers from the jurisdiction of the local bishop. It would make it easier for the superior of the order to move the members to where, in his judgment, they were needed the most. Their constitution, spelling out how they intended to live out their lives, was approved by the pope.

At the time of making the petition to Rome to become a pontifical rite institute, there was not 100 percent agreement among the members of the community of brothers. Some wanted to stay under the jurisdiction of the bishop of Waterford and remain a diocesan rite institute. Those members then split from the Congregation of Christian Brothers and took the name of Presentation Brothers. Their rule of life was modeled after the Presentation Sisters making the necessary adaptations. One of the gifts of that religious order was that the members would have a special devotion to Our Lady under the title of Our Lady of Good Counsel, hence the name Presentation Brothers. However, in 1889 the Presentation Brothers did become a pontifical rite congregation and became exempt from the jurisdiction of the local bishop. Their motto is modeled after the Jesuit motto, *Ad Majorem Dei Gloriam* (For the Greater Glory of God). Presently the Presentation Brothers have foundations in Ireland, England, Canada, West Indies, Ghana, Peru, Nigeria, and Geneva, Switzerland. Therefore, Edmund Ignatius Rice is the recognized founder of two distinct religious order of brothers.

Even to this day, there is a close association between both the Congregation of Christian Brothers and the Presentation Brothers. Most congregations of religious begin as a diocesan rite, and as they expand and grow, they eventually become a pontifical rite congregation. The Christian Brothers have foundations in Ireland, England, and Australia (Melbourne, Sydney, and Brisbane) where they run primary, secondary, and technical schools. Brother Edmund Rice died in 1906 and was beatified by Pope John Paul II on October 6, 1996. Beatification is a step in the process to be declared a saint.

One might ask what the Chalice of Limerick had to do with all of this. Given the context of the severe oppression of the population of Ireland, they would embrace anything that would give them hope. Symbols then such as the chalice of Bishop Turlough O'Brien was a symbol of the sacrifices some had made for their faith. The chalice was a symbol of the Eucharist, and the Eucharist was the reenactment of the Last Supper where Jesus was willing to sacrifice his life to redeem humankind. The chalice then was a tremendous inspiration to the people. Other such artifacts were also in circulation at the time such as the miter of Archbishop Oliver Plunkett, archbishop of Armagh and Primate of Ireland who was martyred on July 1, 1681. The crozier of the bishop of Down and Connor was also in circulation. A crozier is the staff of a bishop and is a symbol of his jurisdiction within his diocese. A crozier is really a shepherd's staff. The crozier of the bishop of Down and Connor could be separated in three parts. That made it easy to transport, and the separated parts could be transported separately. That way, you would not bring attention to the crozier. These artifacts had ways of turning up at different locations in Ireland throughout the Penal Law times. Always they were symbols of courage, faith, and loyalty in the face of persecution.

During the penal times, the deportation of prisoners from England and Ireland was in full swing. This was intended to alleviate overcrowding in jails in Ireland and England. Deportations were either to Tasmania (Van Diemen's Land) or to New South Wales, Australia. New South Wales was founded as a penal colony in 1788. It is estimated that between the years 1788 and 1868, 162,000 prisoners were transported on board 806 ships for either Tasmania or Australia. There was also an attraction for settlers to go to these lands. They could raise sheep there and transport the mutton and wool back to England. The population of settlers in Tasmania grew from 7,000 in 1821 to 24,000 by 1830. The settlers were raising one million sheep.

The settlers and Aborigines were not living peacefully together. Hostilities escalated in the 1820s to the point where the lieutenant governor declared martial law. This gave legal immunity to any settler for killing an Aborigine. In 1830, 2,000 soldiers together with civilians formed a line to drive the Aborigines to a defined reserve. The Aborigines claimed that their hunting grounds were being encroached upon by the settlers.

For these prisoners sent to Tasmania or Australia, it was a life sentence. They would never see their homeland again. There is a song by the Dubliners called "The Fields of Athenry," which captures the mood of these prisoners as they left their homeland. It speaks of the crime of one prisoner who stole corn to feed his starving children, and his sentence was that he was deported on a prison ship bound for Botany Bay, New South Wales, Australia.

Assisting the Irish cause was the War of Independence (1775–1783) in the US. It did have its effects in Ireland. British soldiers were drawn from Ireland to assist the British forces fighting to regain control in the colonies in America. On July 2, 1776, the Continental Congress voted in favor of independence; and on July 4, the delegates adopted the Declaration of Independence, a historic document drafted by Thomas Jefferson. With less forces to protect the land in Ireland, the Irish Parliament felt more vulnerable and less prepared to defend the country.

A large demonstration of Volunteer power took place in Dublin in 1779. Cannons were placed strategically in front of the House of Parliament in Dublin. Placards read, "free trade or this." Their demands were met in December of 1779. Consequently, a large convention of Volunteers was held in Dungarvan in February 1782, demanding a relaxation of penal laws against Catholics. In the meantime, the French Revolution was taking place in France in 1789, with its emphasis on liberty, equality, and fraternity. Irish people were aware of what was going on in the continent. It gave confidence to the Catholics of Ireland. This led to the Catholic Relief Act 1793 which gave Catholics a right to vote. They could also attend Dublin University. However, Catholics could not become a member of Parliament, nor could they become a judge. Further concessions followed in 1795 with the establishment of Maynooth Seminary for the training of future priests to serve in Ireland.

THE EFFECTS OF THE
GREAT FAMINE

Farmworkers during the Great Famine, 1845

Things were beginning to change for Ireland. The first of a series of Catholic Relief Acts were passed in 1778. This act allowed Catholics to join the British Army. They could purchase land if they took the Oath of Allegiance. This was first approved by the British Parliament, and the Irish Parliament followed suit. The Catholic Relief Act of 1791 was broader in scope. By this act, Catholics could practice law. They could exercise their religion with some reservations such as chapels and schools could be built but teachers and priests had to be registered with the state. The ringing of bells to announce a service was still forbidden. Priests could not wear vestments when officiating at a liturgy or celebrate Mass in the open air. Monastic orders were still forbidden, and no endowment could be made to any Catholic school or college. The Catholic Relief Act of 1793 allowed Catholics to vote. These relief acts made life a little more tolerable for the people. However, there would still be some dark days ahead.

With the passage of time, the Irish people had lost so much. They owned only about 5 percent of the land. They had become totally dependent on one crop—the potato. The potato had always been a reliable crop for the people of Ireland. An acre of potatoes could feed a family of six for a whole year. It is an easy crop to grow and nutritious and can be cooked in a variety of ways. It is a good source of protein, nitrogen, iron, calcium, chorine, and potassium. However, the law of nature, being what it is, is no one can depend solely on one crop.

The Great Famine began in 1845 and lasted four years. It had drastic consequences for the people of Ireland. The potato blight had affected the whole continent. For example, England, Scotland, Wales, France, Germany, Belgium, the Netherlands, Spain, and even Russia suffered the blight; but in no other country was the effect the same. Only in Ireland did the people undergo the Great Famine. The saddest part of the story was it did not have to take place. It could have been easily avoided if the British Parliament had responded as they should have.

Still today, an estimated 25 percent of the world's population go to bed hungry. It is not that there is not enough food to go around. There is plenty of food. The problem is the distribution of food, and that is where politics plays a role. It was the same in Ireland during the Great Famine. Two-thirds of the soil in Ireland that could be cultivated was given over to barley, wheat, and oats. All of this was exported to England every year. Each year of the famine, enough food was being exported that would feed 12 million people. Also, being exported were pigs, poultry, and eggs. For the most part, the peasantry in Ireland did not eat meat because they could not afford it. They sold meat and poultry to pay the rent which was due twice a year. Added to this was the tithe owed to the Anglican Church. During the famine years, hundreds of thousands of peasant farmers and laborers were evicted from their homes.

The export of grain and meat continued to England during this time. During the famine, many of the migrants going to Canada and the US died en route. Because so many people had been evicted from their homes, there was more land available to raise pigs and cattle, and all of these were being exported from Ireland at a time when people were dying of starvation.

Death by starvation is not pleasant by any means. When the intake of food is cut off from the body, the body goes into a defensive mode to protect itself. However, the reality is the body slowly eats itself. It recognizes that food is scarce, and it begins to relocate what it can in preparation. First, the body begins to consume the fat tissue available to it. When all the fat has been exhausted, it turns to the muscle tissue. Then the heart rate slows down as well as the breathing. The immune system is compromised, and there is an increased susceptibility to disease and infections. Dehydration can be a factor. Usually, death results from some infection or other. Any prolonged starvation can do severe damage to vital body organs. It is estimated that one million people died of starvation or typhus. An estimated two million migrated. Some died en route.

People who lived close to coastal areas seemed to do better because they could scrounge for seafood such as periwinkles, barnacles, limpets, crabs, and edible seaweed. The coastal fishermen had access to the sea and could catch all the different species of fish such as mackerel, dogfish, etc. However, the curragh used were fragile and could not fish deep waters. Over time, even the fishermen had to forfeit their fishing equipment to pay the rent.

As days passed into weeks and weeks into months, people became more and more despondent. Evicted families had no place to go for the most part. Some stayed around their former homes for days. It was hard for them to leave. Their parents and grandparents had been born in that same home, and there was so much family history there. After being evicted, their homes were torn down by the evicting soldiers for non-payment of rent. British soldiers serving in Ireland found it hard to evict the poor from their homes. Landlords then hired thugs to do the dirty work for them.

Then scurvy showed its ugly head. With a deficiency of vitamin C, bleeding ulcers appeared in the gums, mouth, and throat. Scurvy became widespread all over the country. People lost the will to live and prayed for death.

News of the great famine spread to the United States. An appeal was made for help from the US Government. Senator Henry Clay of Kentucky made a passionate plea for relief for Ireland in 1847. Senator John Crittenden presented the bill to the senate on February 26, 1847. During the debate on the bill before the senate, pleas were made not to be disrespectful to England. Simultaneously, reports were being made by the American Consul in Dublin and London regarding the famine in Ireland. The problem was that politics was clouding the real issue. The consuls saw it as an opportunity to increase the exports from the US especially of surplus Indian corn. Henry Clay was successful in presenting a bill before the senate for relief, and after much consultation, the bill did pass the senate and the house and was signed by President James Polk. Incidentally, he was of Scotch Irish descent.

The official government relief effort however had little "teeth" in it. Only two ships were destined to make the journey from the US to Ireland. The USS *Jamestown* sailed from Boston to Cork carrying relief. The USS *Macedonian* was to sail from New York. In all, the American government relief fund was in the range of $500,000. Private relief efforts were in the millions of dollars. In all, it is estimated that 118 vessels carried relief to Irish ports. Relief came from all kinds of unexpected sources such as the Choctaw Indians, who themselves had experienced severe deprivation and knew and understood the plight of the Irish and donated $170. It might have been the widow's mite, but it came from a generous heart. Another unexpected source included the sultan of Ottoman Empire, the Jewish community of New York, and the Committee of Colored Citizens, Philadelphia. Archbishop Hughes of New York continued to make passionate pleas for the starving Irish. He was instrumental in organizing much of the relief that came from the East Coast. While vessels were approaching Irish coastal ports, other ships laden with wheat, barley, oats, and meat were leaving the country bound for British ports. It is estimated that 80,000 tons of food came to the Irish ports during the Great Famine.

Thousands of Irish began to cross the Irish Sea to England in search of work. Many of the people who made the crossing were themselves poor, destitute, emaciated, and near death. The English economy was also in poor shape, and England had its own economic woes to content with. Charles Trevelyan, the prime minister in 1847, held that the landlords in Ireland should solve the problems of the poor in Ireland and not depend on a bailout from England. The British Parliament enacted the Irish Poor Law Extension Act in June of 1847. It did not solve the problem; instead it exacerbated it. Starving people scrounged around seeking whatever they could eat. Items eaten were wild blackberries, nettles, turnips, old cabbage leaves, edible seaweed, roots, and even grass. Parents had to listen to starving children crying from hunger pains, and yet they were unable to satisfy their hunger. The people who died were buried without coffins, mostly in shallow graves which could be ravaged by dogs, cats, and rats. Relief would not be offered to people who owned more than a quarter acre of land without that person forfeiting the ownership of land to get food from the soup kitchens.

The relief efforts of the British government were inadequate. The government spent £8 million in relief in 1845. Three million people were receiving relief from the soup kitchens. The Soup Kitchens Act of 1847 called for the daily distribution of soup. It was to be financed by the Irish landowners and merchants. The landowners were themselves not receiving payments from the tenants who occupied their land and could not contribute then to the soup kitchen. Soup kitchens began in the spring of 1847. The soup provided by the soup kitchen was made from two-thirds Indian corn and one-third rice. Each person served was given a quart of soup and a piece of bread. Over time, this would not provide all the nutrients the body needed. It is estimated that the soup cost two pennies per serving. However, it was weak of nutritional value, but at least it was warm.

The potato crop harvested in the fall of 1847 was only one quarter of the normal potato crop. There were reasons for this. The seed potatoes were themselves diseased, and the blight was still there. Other crops such as cabbage, beans, and peas were above the price range of the poor farmer. The winter brought more sleet, snow, and rain. The price of purchasing potatoes soared, and as a result, the poor again could not afford to buy potatoes.

Evicted people could go to the workhouses. However, these workhouses had poor sanitation and little heating during the winter months. The workhouses provided a shelter and not much more. Some of the workhouses were formerly warehouses, converted for the purpose of housing indigent people.

The statistics from this period of Irish history are staggering. The population fell from 8.4 million in 1844 to 6.6 million in 1851. An estimated 2 million migrated, many of them dying en route to their destination. It is estimated that 1 million died of starvation or typhus. The population of Ireland today is 4.9 million. The story of the Great Famine is a sad and painful story. It is a story that could have been avoided had the proper government agencies realistically and truthfully addressed the problems.

THE LANDLORD

Not all the stories coming from this time were bad. There were some good and concerned landlords as the following story illustrates. John Dwyer, a peasant farmer, lived in Coonagh, about three miles from Limerick. He had lost his small farm because he was in arrears in paying his rent to the landlord. He had to seek work as a farm laborer to keep a roof over his wife and fifteen-year-old son. At the time, it was customary to go to the town square to seek employment. John went to Limerick City. Landlords who were seeking to employ able-bodied workers would go to the town square and negotiate with a prospective worker. Arrangements would be made to work for a day, a week, or a month depending on the need.

John was not hired, and he knew that his family would be without food that day. As he was on his way home, a carriage passed him. A wealthy looking man stepped out and asked John if he was looking for work. He responded yes. The man offered him a job at £1 a week for a whole year. He would also provide room and board. This was a godsend. Normally, the pay of a laborer was less than a £1 a week, and this offer included room and board. The wealthy landowner gave him instructions on how to get to his estate, which was about twenty miles away, in Ennis. He would have to walk there. The wealthy man told John that he was to present himself to the butler upon arriving at the estate in Ennis, and he would show him to his room and give

39

him his instructions as to his responsibilities. In the meantime, his wife and son would remain in Coonagh.

He said a quick goodbye to his wife and son. In the meantime, his wife, Joanne, had secured a job as a maid in a wealthy estate near Limerick. Arriving in Ennis, he was shown to his room and given his instructions. John's responsibilities were to sow thirty acres of barley and thirty acres of wheat. It took him a whole year. At the end of the year, he went into the landlord to be paid. The landlord paid him out £50. John was so excited. Then the landlord made him a proposition. He told him that if he worked for another year, he would give him an extra bonus of another £50. That meant at the end of the second year, he would receive £150. This meant that every day he worked, he would be paid double. It was extremely generous. For the second year, his responsibilities were to build a racecourse as the landowner had racehorses. It would take him a year to complete the project. At the end of the second year, he went to the landlord to be paid. The landlord counted out £150.

John picked up the money and was about to leave when the landlord said, "I have another proposition to make to you. I want you to renovate my home. I need new windows, roof, staircase, etc. It will take you a whole year. At the end of that time, I will pay you £250."

Again, this was a most generous offer. John worked for a year and completed the project. He went in to be paid, and the landlord counted out £250. John accepted the money. He was excited about going home and meeting with his wife and son again.

Before he left the landlord's office, the landlord said to him. "John you have been a good employee, and if in the future I have work for you, I will send for you. Right now, I have none. However, I will make you a proposition. You have your money, and you can go. Or I will give you three bits of advice. You cannot take both."

John thought for a moment. *The landlord has been good to me. He has treated me right.*

Maybe, this advice will lead John to more money. John decided to take the advice. He gave the landlord back the £250.

The landlord said, "Your first bit of advice is not to go through the village of New Market on Fergus on your way home." (New Market on Fergus is about five miles from Ennis, and he would pass through it on his way to Limerick. The landlord suggested bypassing the village altogether).

John looked at the landlord in surprise.

John said to him, "Listen, I am paying good money for this advice, and your first piece of advice is nonsense. Your second piece of advice better be good."

The landlord said, "Your second piece of advice is not to stay overnight in any house on your way home."

This infuriated John.

He responded to the landlord, "You cannot be serious. I am paying you all this money, and your second piece of advice is ridiculous. Your third bit of advice better be good."

With that, the landlord said, "Things are not always what they seem to be."

Now the landlord had John's full attention. John was livid with rage.

He turned to the landlord and said to him: "I worked hard these past three years for you. I have been a faithful worker. I never missed a day's work. You have taken advantage of me. You never intended to pay me, and you had me on a string all along. I will tell everyone I meet how you treated me."

With that, John walked out.

The landlord called after him, "John, drop by the kitchen and get a loaf of bread to eat for the journey home."

John thought to himself, *That is the most expensive loaf of bread I have ever bought.*

With that, John went by the kitchen, and the cook gave him the loaf of bread.

He started his twenty-mile journey home. He had only gone a short distance when he encountered two other workers making their way to Limerick, also. He joined them. They each had worked for a year, and both had £40 to show for their efforts. They were sharing with each other what they intended to do with the money. As they approached New Market on Fergus, John was about to go with them when he remembered his first bit of advice: *Do not go through the village of New Market on Fergus*. He made up an excuse saying he wanted to be alone. He promised to walk quickly. He asked if they would wait for him at the other side of New Market on Fergus. When he had walked around, he found they were not there. He waited an hour. A passerby asked John if he had heard the news.

John responded, "What news?"

The passerby told John that two men had been beaten up and robbed as they passed through the village just an hour ago. John was glad he had taken his first bit of advice. John was curious as to why the landlord knew it would have been risky to go through the village of New Market on Fergus. He surmised he must have a good reason.

He decided he needed to move on from New Market on Fergus as quickly as possible and get on the road again. It was now beginning to get dark. There were no streetlights to show the way, and he was having difficulty seeing where he was going. He saw a light in a farmer's house, and he went there. He asked the lady of the house if he could stay the night in the barn. All he asked for was some tea as he had the loaf of bread. She invited him to share dinner. He had accepted the invitation when he heard a voice from the bedroom asking who was there.

The lady of the house responded, "There is nobody here. I am talking to myself."

Then she whispered to John that her husband who was in the bedroom was a paraplegic. He had fallen from a horse a year before and was bedridden. After dinner, she invited him to stay the night in the guest room. John remembered his second bit of advice: *Don't stay overnight in any house on your way home*.

John told the lady that he would rather sleep in the barn, and on the first light of day, he would be on his way. The lady insisted. And John did not want to hurt her feelings, so he accepted her offer. He went into the guest room. He intended to slip out the window while she was asleep and go to the barn. While he was waiting for her to go to bed, he heard voices outside his window. He listened. He recognized the voice of the lady but not the man she was talking with. They were plotting to murder the paraplegic and put the blame on John. He waited a few more minutes and got out the window and headed for home. He walked all night long.

He arrived at Coonagh, his home, at 8:00 a.m. just three miles from Limerick. He looked in the kitchen window and saw his wife with another man. This was the last straw. He grabbed a stick at the back door and rushed into the kitchen. He was about to strike the man when he remembered his third bit of advice: *Things are not always what they appear to be.*

He screamed, "Who is this man!"

His wife answered, "He is your only son, John. He was fifteen when you left home, and he is eighteen now and fully grown."

John was glad he had taken the third bit of advice and not struck his own son.

He sat down and was sharing with his wife and son all that had happened to him in the intervening three years and how the landlord had given him three bits of advice and how the advice had saved his life. Suddenly there was a knock at the door. John's wife opened the door, and there were two detectives there asking about the whereabouts of John. He was arrested and charged with the murder of the paraplegic. He was brought to court and tried for the crime and found guilty. It was an open-and-shut case. The murder weapon (a knife) had been found in the guest room. He had used the knife to eat his dinner at the paraplegic's home.

There was something about the judge. He had seen him somewhere before, but he was not sure. The judge asked John if he had anything to declare before sentence was pronounced, and John again professed his innocence.

Then the judge took off his white wig and declared to the court: "That man's story is true. I am the one who gave him the three bits of advice. He worked for me for three years and he is a good man."

Then John recognized the judge. He had been the employee of the landlord for three years, and the landlord was also a judge. John reflected: *Maybe that is how he knew it was dangerous to go through New Market on Fergus. He must have heard of reports of stealing from passersby.*

John went to thank the judge for saving his life again.

Then the judge asked him a question. "What happened to the loaf of bread that you got from the kitchen before beginning your journey home?"

John responded, "It is still at home."

The judge told him to go home and eat the loaf of bread. John rushed home. He got a knife and cut into the bread. There was a small box inside the bread. John opened the box and there was £250. There is justice in this world, and there are some good people in it. John's faith in the goodness of some people was restored that day. With the £250, John was now able to buy some land again and to become an independent farmer which was his life's dream.

It would be wrong to say that all landlords were bad. There were some kind-hearted landlords who had a lot of compassion and did not throw their tenants off the land for non-payment of their rent. Rather, they allowed them to stay on the land. After all, the landlords were not the ones who created the problem. The problem was the blight of the potato for three successive years and the inability of the government to respond to the needs of their constituents. In the last analysis, the government exists to serve the needs of the people.

THE AFTERMATH OF
THE GREAT FAMINE

Cathedral of the Assumption, Thurles, built 1879

St. Patrick's College, Thurles, built 1837

Colleen Bawn

It would take an impoverished land time to recover from the horrible disaster of the Great Famine. In 1849, the Encumbered Estates Act was passed by the British Parliament. Huge estates of land in Ireland were in heavy debt and unable to pay rent. The Encumbered Estates Act was an effort to cut the red tape and make it easier to sell such holdings. Land prices tumbled to a new low. Land could be purchased for a fraction of its real value. Fortune seekers mainly from England took advantage of the opportunity to make a profit. However, after buying the land, they raised the rent on the already impoverished tenants. In a period of the next five years, 50,000 new tenants were evicted.

How much more could the Irish people take? There came a light at the end of the tunnel. There is power in numbers. Charles Stewart Parnell founded the Land League. It was a national alliance which was founded in County Mayo on October 21, 1879. Its primary aim was to end the concept of landlordism in Ireland. Another concern of the Land League was to work toward free sale of land, fixity of tenure, and fair rent. It was heavily funded by organizations in the US committed to helping the cause of Ireland especially the Ancient Order of Hibernians which was founded in New York in 1836. Members were themselves Irish immigrants or descendants of immigrants. In Ireland, the Land League defiantly burned land leases and blocked evictions in process, much to the chagrin of the more notorious landlords.

This led to the passing of the Land Act of 1881. This act brought about the reductions in rents owed. It also recognized the interest tenants had in their leased farms and improvements that they had made to the land they occupied. This was followed by Wyndham Act, 1903, which provided government-guaranteed loans in the purchase of land for tenant farmers buying from landlords. A great deal of the credit for this change is undoubtedly due to Charles Steward Parnell.

He was born June 27, 1846, during the Great Famine. His family was Anglo-Irish. He was educated at Cambridge University and served as a member of Parliament, 1875–1891. He went to the US and addressed the House of Representatives on February 2, 1880, to speak on the needs of the Irish. He then went on a tour of sixty-two cities in the US and Canada and was dubbed "the uncrowned king of Ireland."

The power of the Land League spread like a wildfire throughout all of Ireland. People took notice of its effectiveness and the fact that there is power in numbers as the following story will illustrate.

Charles Cunningham Boycott was born on March 12, 1832, in England. He was a soldier in the British Army and went to serve in Ireland. After his tenure in the army, he became a land agent. The local members of the Land League persuaded the employees of Boycott to refuse to work for him so as to isolate him. Local merchants of the village of Ballinrobe, County Mayo, refused to serve him in their stores. Boycott protested in a letter to *The Times* of this unjust infraction of his rights as a citizen and claimed he was a "loyal servant of the realm." The Times sent reporters to investigate what was happening. Fifty Orangemen from County Cavan and County Monaghan came to his rescue to harvest the crops on Lord Erne's estate for which Boycott was responsible. To protect the fifty Orangemen, one thousand of the Royal Irish Constabulary were deployed to the scene. It costs to the government £10,000 to provide protection, and the harvest was worth £500. This incident got so much publicity that the word *boycott* entered the English language.

Incidents like this gave great courage and hope to the Irish people. They began to recognize that if they united, they had a political clout and they could make demands against unjust laws. Probably the two most striking events that influenced the turn of the tide for the people of Ireland were the Catholic Emancipation which was passed in 1829 and the formation of the Land League in 1879 and the passing of the Land Act in 1881.

Another influence in these changing times was the fact that the population of Ireland was becoming more educated. They had their own schools. They had access to university education. They took pride in their heritage. Also, they had freedom to practice their faith. It was a time of renaissance. St. Patrick's College-Maynooth was established in 1795 by the Maynooth College Act for the training of seminarians. St. Patrick's College-Thurles was founded in 1837 initially as a lay college and seminary. From 1902 to 1988, it was exclusively a seminary. Beautiful church buildings began to spring up all over the country. I will just name a few: St. John's Cathedral in Limerick was built of limestone, 1852–1882. The Franciscan Church Limerick was built 1876–1886. The Redemptorist Church in Mount St. Alphonsus, Limerick, was built in 1853. The Cathedral of the Assumption in Thurles was opened in 1879. St. Michael Church in Limerick was originally destroyed during the Siege of Limerick in 1651 and was rebuilt in its present site in 1801. The present Pro-Cathedral of St. Mary in Dublin was built in 1825, and the Cathedral of St. Mary and St. Anne in Cork was dedicated in 1808. Some of the funding for these buildings undoubtedly came from the Irish who had migrated from the country and were sensitive to the needs of the land of their birth. Moreover, it is true to say that the average congregant of the churches made huge sacrifices. One way they looked at their donations was the fact that the congregants accepted the fact they would never have much of the world's goods to call their own. Nevertheless, their churches belonged to them, and they would visit these churches with great pride, knowing the sacrifices they had made to make the buildings a reality.

When the people saw objects like the Chalice of Limerick, they were reminded of the tremendous sacrifices made by their own bishops and priests, despite all odds, to keep the faith alive among the people. Some of them gave their lives. More than anything else, it was the indomitable and resilient will of the stubborn Irish people who would never give up and resisted for years the Penal Laws imposed upon them. With the Catholic Emancipation Act 1829, people were free to worship in public again.

One story about this time in Irish history is the story of the Colleen Bawn or, in Gaelic, *Cailín Bán*. Colleen Bawn literally means the innocent girl. It is the story of a brutal murder of a girl who was just shy of her sixteenth birthday. The news of her brutal death rocked the nation. Her name was Ellen Hanley. She was indeed a beauty queen. Her mother died when Ellen was young, and she was raised by her Uncle John Connery of Garryowen, Limerick. There have been so many books and plays written about the Colleen Bawn it is hard to know where the truth is and what is fiction. One play of note is the *Brides of Garryowen*, which was first performed in New York on March 27, 1860.

I recall as a ten-year-old my father sharing the story with me of the Colleen Bawn. The basic facts of the story are as follows: John Shanley who was in his twenties and from the village of Croom, County Limerick, met and fell in love with Ellen Hanley of Garryowen, Limerick. It was a whirlwind romance. The two lovers eloped from her uncle's home and allegedly were married by a priest in Limerick. It was questioned later whether the priest was legitimate or not. There was no record of any marriage, either civil or religious, ever found. Some claim that the minister was not a legitimate one and that John Shanley cajoled her into marrying him and used a substitute for a priest. After the alleged marriage, Ellen was rejected by the Shanley family, and within less than a week, John Shanley had gotten tired of Ellen. In the meantime, it was alleged that John's mother was in the process of arranging a marriage of her son to a wealthy lady. It seems that the Shanley family were nearly broke, and this arranged marriage would change that reality.

John Shanley devised a plot to kill his new bride. They had been married only six weeks. He requested the aid of the family servant, Stephen Sullivan, to complete his mission. John cajoled Ellen to go with him on a romantic trip by yacht from Foynes, County Limerick, to Kilrush, County Clare, on the other side of the Shannon River which was about twenty miles away.

They were scheduled to leave Foynes on July 14, 1819, at 6:00 p.m. They would have a romantic dinner on the yacht and leisurely spend a beautiful evening sailing into the sunset. While the actual distance is only seventeen miles, one has to take into consideration the tidal flow. On this night, the tide was coming in. Also, there was the usual westerly breeze which would necessitate much tacking and beating of the sailboat.

The original plot was to throw Ellen overboard during the evening. Ellen could not swim. As to what exactly happened on board that yacht that evening is anybody's guess. We do know she was drowned. We do know that she put up a brave fight. Her drowning took place around midnight. Horrific screams were heard at both sides of the River Shannon from 11:30 p.m. to midnight. Then the screams stopped. The location in the river where the foul crime was committed is at least four miles wide. The silence of the night was rudely interrupted by her screams which would have carried a long distance. Screams were heard in Tarbert, County Kerry, and in Killimer, County Clare. Her body was washed ashore six weeks later at Moneypoint near the town of Killimer, County Clare. Patrick O'Connell was the farmer who found her and had her buried in his plot at the cemetery at Burrane near Killimer. The epitaph on the tombstone read: "Here lies the Colleen Bawn, murdered on the Shannon River, July 14, 1819." Over time, souvenir hunters chipped away the tombstone, and there is no trace of the original left. The tombstone that marks the grave today is that of Patrick O'Connell.

As to what happened on that fatal night on the River Shannon is open to interpretation. Ellen did put up a brave fight for her life. When they found her body, there were bruises on her ankles. It seems that they weighed the body down tying a rope around her ankles which was attached to the boat anchor. The anchor was missing from the boat. When found, her body was naked.

It is conjectured that John Shanley and Stephen Sullivan first threw her overboard. Somehow or other, she grabbed on to the punt boat which was being pulled behind the yacht and climbed aboard. She began to scream for help. She continued to scream all the while the culprits tried to get her back on board the yacht again. She was aware they had murder in their hearts and there was no turning back. Eventually when they got her back on board the yacht, they stripped her naked. They weighted the body down with the anchor and again threw her overboard.

Allegedly they sailed on to Kilrush that night and put the word out the following morning that Helen had accidentally fallen overboard and drowned. Word had quickly spread in the Kilrush community about the horrific screams that were heard the night before and lasting for thirty minutes in the vicinity of Killimer not far from Kilrush. A search went on for weeks to locate the body of the Colleen Bawn. The issue was resolved when the body came ashore in Moneypoint, near Killimer, six weeks later. John Shanley was first arrested and tried for the horrific crime which had caught national attention. John's mother wanted the best possible defense barrister to represent him. Daniel O'Connell, who later became the famous liberator of Ireland, was chosen to represent John Shanley. The trial took place in Limerick City and lasted several days. John was found guilty and sentenced to death by hanging. The execution took place in Gallows Green on the Clare side of the river close to the city of Limerick. Stephen Sullivan evaded arrest for three months; but he was eventually caught, tried, and found guilty and was also hanged in the same Gallows Green.

There was a lot of pretrial publicity and during the trial itself of John Shanley. People speculated whether the Shanley family could afford to hire a barrister of law of such esteem as Daniel O'Connell. One of the stories was that at the time, John Shanley' s mother was in possession of the Bishop O'Brien chalice and she offered the chalice to Daniel O'Connell as part of the payment for his services and he accepted it. When the trial was over, Daniel O'Connell decided to give the chalice to the bishop of Limerick at the time.

The Chalice of Limerick which had been the chalice of Bishop Turlough O'Brien and had been making the rounds in many different locations during the penal times was now showing signs of the wear. The original gold plate had been worn away. The chalice was now more of historical and sentimental value than anything else. The bishop of Limerick, Charles Touhy, decided that since the chalice had been in fact sold to Daniel O'Connell, it had lost its consecration as a chalice. Rather than refurbish it and have it reconsecrated, he decided to bury the chalice in the burial place of its rightful owner, Bishop Turlough O'Brien who had given his life in martyrdom in 1651 during the Siege of Limerick. The final resting place of the Chalice of Limerick is now with its rightful owner, interred with the remains of Bishop Turlough O'Brien.

CONCLUSION

The penal times were hard times for the people of Ireland. Nevertheless, they were also revealing times. They especially showed the resilience and audaciousness of a people to survive against all odds. They held on to their faith and were willing to die for it, if necessary. They made the sacrifices they were called on to make.

A special thanks to the martyrs of those times who made the ultimate sacrifice of their lives. Father Robert Southwall, an English poet and writer, was arrested while celebrating Mass in England in 1592. He was executed for treason in 1595. Sir Thomas More who was chancellor of England during the reign of King Henry VIII was executed in the Tower of London, July 6, 1535. Following the Siege of Drogheda, the priests and civilians who took refuge in the steeple of St. Peter's Church were burned alive on September 10, 1649. The remaining priests in the city were clubbed to death. At the end of the Siege of Limerick on October 27, 1651, the mayor of the city, Dominic Fannon, was drawn, quartered, and decapitated. Bishop Turlough O'Brien was hanged the same day.

The Chalice of Limerick is a historical novel aimed at highlighting that resilience in times of persecution. While people had little, they had their faith. Small and insignificant faith symbols such as a chalice of a martyred bishop, were reminders to them of the sacrifices that others had made for them.

Our gratitude also to the political leaders who brought about change, especially our gratitude to Daniel O'Connell, who was responsible for the Catholic Emancipation Act 1829. Our thanks go to Charles Steward Parnell for the formation of the Land League in 1878 and his efforts to lead the Irish Parliamentary Party, 1888–1891. These leaders gave a nation a hope and a vision for the future.

God hears the cry of the oppressed. (Psalm 10:18)

ABOUT THE AUTHOR

Monsignor Michael Flannery is a retired priest of the Jackson Diocese, Mississippi. He took up the art of writing in his retirement. His first book, *The Saltillo Mission,* is about a mission in Saltillo, Mexico, jointed sponsored by the Diocese of Jackson and the Diocese of Biloxi. His second book, *The Prankster Priest* is about the art of pulling pranks. His third book, *Padre's Christian Stories* is a collection of Christian Stories, his fourth book, *St. Anthony's Eagles,* concerns the habits of eagles. Other books by the same author which are presently being prepared for publication by Covenant Books are: *One View of the Holy Grail, The Emerald, In Search of my Twin, Rubies Lead to Adventure, and Father Unknown.*

CPSIA information can be obtained
at www.ICGtesting.com
Printed in the USA
BVHW061226030321
601537BV00009B/168

9 781636 307060